Well, That Didn't Work

Hard Lessons Learned In Love & Marriage

By

David E. Goodin

3J2 Publishing Group, LLC
Stockbridge, GA

Dedication

This Book is dedicated to my loving wife, Cynthia who has been with me through many trials and transitions over the past thirty- three years and to whom I am very thankful. Also, to our chil- dren who have been there for us through the many seasons of my life including, the good, bad and the ugly. I thank them all that after struggling through much of their upbringing they gave me another chance to win over their love and respect. Lastly, to the single parent households and children who grew up in single parent households I hope they may find some nuggets of wisdom and direction from a from a Father they may have never had.

REMEMBER, MOST PEOPLE END UP IN A BAD
RELATIONSHIP BECAUSE WHEN THEY FIRST MET SOMEONE,

THEY ACTED LIKE THEY DIDN'T SEE WHAT THEY SAW,
AND ACTED LIKE THEY DIDN'T HEAR WHAT THEY HEARD.
PEOPLE WILL ALWAYS SHOW YOU WHAT YOU WILL HAVE TO
DEAL WITH ONCE YOU GET INTO A RELATIONSHIP WITH THEM.

MAKE SURE YOU STAY OUT OF THE DENIAL OF WHAT THEY ARE REALLY
SHOWING YOU ABOUT THEMSELVES. PAY ATTENTION TO DETAILS.
THE DIFFERENCE BETWEEN YOUR BEING HAPPY OR HEARTBROKEN WILL BE IN YOUR ABILITY
TO READ BETWEEN THE LINES OF WHAT YOU HEAR AND SEE RIGHT BEFORE YOUR EYES.

Table of Contents

Introduction

The effects of growing up without your father even though he lived just five minutes away.

Five years ago, I stopped in Xenia, Ohio where I was born. I went to clean out a storage my stepmother and my father had who had passed a few years earlier.

They said there were some things in there that belonged to my father and his parents, which were my grandparents, and they thought I might want to have them.

Of course, I was excited to get what they had. It was jewelry, papers and a couple hundred pictures that went back to my great great grandparents.

Wow!!!

I couldn't wait to get back home to Florida to go through them. When I got to Jacksonville and got settled I took the boxes out on the screened in patio and with great excitement began to go through the pictures and boxes.

It had my grandparents wedding rings, and a lot of her jewelry, pictures of my Father from about four years old all the way until a few years before his death when he was eighty-one.

I saw pictures of my half-sister who passed a few years ago. I had a great relationship with her even though we didn't meet until she was in her twenties. I also saw pictures of my half-brother that I may have come across once or twice in life, he also passed a couple years ago.

I saw pictures of my Father with them both at graduations and events at my grandparents.

THEN IT HIT ME AFTER GOING THROUGH A HUNDRED PICTURES!!!!!!!!!!!!!!!!

I WASN'T IN ANY OF THEM AND UNTIL I WAS NINE YEARS OLD, I LIVED JUST FIVE MINUTES AWAY!!!!!!!

I put the boxes down quickly and said to myself, THAT IS NOT MY FAMILY, I AM AN ANDERSON!!!!

I thought about how sharp everyone looked in the pictures and how well off they all were while my mother and I were struggling.

I thought how I didn't have very good clothes to wear to school and a teacher in third grade gave me a D in hygiene.

The only toys I had were Popsicle sticks to race when there was water flowing down the street to a drain and five minutes away they had everything a family could want.

My Father never ever came to pick me up. I left the boxes there overnight and the thought hit me, it's too much history to keep from my children if they would need it so I went through the rest and put it up.

The rest will be in my book, The Greatest Story I Ever Saw; Which Is the Story Of Me.

CHAPTER ONE
Relationships

Here's the truth, you may not want to hear...

A real man will reflect back on the pain and devastation he inflicted on women, who truly loved them. They'll feel great shame and remorse and try to help other men from doing the same.

Sometimes we as men will meet a young woman with a promising future and totally train wreck her life with little concern of what we're actually doing to someone who actually cares about us.

I've been married to Cynthia, (who approved this post), for 32 years, but about 13 years before I met her I met a young lady at my job who was 19 and in college on her way to getting a degree and I started dating her even though I was going through a divorce. I moved in with her and shortly afterwards my divorce was final.

I was always seeing someone else while I was with her. I'd be at another woman's house with her car and she would come pick it up and leave.

She didn't think she could get pregnant, but she did and I talked her into have an abortion even though she in no way wanted to; I pressed so hard she did it and never got pregnant again before she passed. I had multiple relationships with other women while living with her and I know she knew it.

She was a stunningly beautiful lady that always had other guys trying to get with her, but she said to me one day,

Her heart is broken because even though she could literally have any man she wants, the only man she wanted, wants any and every other woman but her and she never dreamed when she met me she'd end up in the emotional state that she was in.

Not long after that conversation one night while we were laying in the bed, I got up and got a few clothes and said I was leaving and walked to my car on a cold night with freezing temperatures. She followed me to the car in a housecoat and asked me what was I doing and I told her I was leaving and left her stunned. I never went back, I just moved on to the next woman.

I so wish I could say this was the only time I did something like this but the truth is it was just one of many, sad to say.

Maybe this is why my heart is towards helping men, both married and single get the right attitude and reverence for women and especially our young ones before they do irreparable damage to them if they haven't already. We as men must do better and my life is now dedicated to helping us men realize who we really are as protectors of our daughters, wives and women as a whole instead destroyers of their self-worth, potential and self-esteem.

Most men are foolish in their youth and leave a trail of bad decisions with long lasting consequences that also affect many children, but at some point, he must transition from a boy to a man.

That David Goodin has been dead for almost thirty-three years because one night I gave my life to the Lord and he filled me with the Holy Spirit and for some reason I didn't think the same or want to do things like I was used to doing. I used to trip off myself wondering what was going on with me.

Here are some relationship passages, quotes, and truths I've learned along the way. They'll keep you from a lot of heartache and save you from yourself

When you meet someone, you feel you would like to get into a relationship with but you really don't trust somethings about them, STOP RIGHT THERE. You don't go forward into a relationship with someone that you don't trust, let alone consider for marriage. Trust is the very thing that will MAKE OR BRAKE A RELATIONSHIP. Don't jump off a cliff and say, I'll grow wings on the way down

- Here's a tip.

Your spouse, boyfriend or girlfriend can still experience things with you that no one ever did, even if it's not the first time you've been married or in a relationship!!

This is not as complicated as one might think. You can start by going to restaurants you never went to with anyone else.

- Go see movies that you never seen with anyone else.

- Go on a cruise to a place you never went

- Fly to a city you never flew to

- Fix some meals you never fixed for anyone

- Ride in a car that you've never rode in with anyone.

- Live in an apartment or house that you've never lived in with anyone

- Sleep in a bed that you've never slept in with anyone

- Go see some family that you've never visited with anyone

- Go see some friends that you never visited with anyone

- Have you ever had flowers delivered?

- Have you ever given someone a card at dinner or just because?

The point is, talk about things you can do together that neither of you have ever done with anyone else and start making exclusive memories together.

P.S. Don't take any past events the two of you may have had in the past personal and you can start to have something really good together.

- A couple in premarital counseling was asked to look at their fiancée in their eyes and tell them why they loved them so much and why they want to marry them. After saying wonderful things about the kind of person they were I told them everything they said about the other was moving, and those things were enough to get them married, but not enough to keep them married. I wanted to hear how well they found they processed through conflicts. That will determine more of where you are headed as a couple and their chances of success in the marriage.

- WHY ARE YOU ALWAYS TRYING TO CONTROL MY LIFE AND TELL ME WHAT TO DO??? Sometimes when a man or woman is always trying to advise their wife or husband on some things that would make things easier for them and their intentions are as simple as that, they will find out one of two things by their spouses' response. They will either wonder, why are you always trying to control my life?????

Or they will think they have the greatest man or woman on the planet because they're always looking out for them and trying to make their life easy. Being able to discern and know the difference between the two and which one you have will keep you from being discouraged while thinking you were just trying to be considerate and caring. So many husbands and wives have gifts they can't even recognize or benefit from because in most cases that strong response is out of past filters from old relationships. In most cases when a person lashes out at you for trying to help, they are not talking to you, but someone in their past that was controlling.

In many cases, as sad as it is, The Abused becomes the Abuser to someone who would never do to them what others have done to them because they truly want to love and care for them like no one in their past was willing to do. Appreciate what you have before it becomes what you had and someone else appreciates what you had.

- Most times in a relationship one person gives more than the other and wants to provide any desire that comes from their spouses' lips and anyone would definitely be blessed to have someone like that in their life.

- One of the main reasons people who have people like this in their lives and they never returned the love, attention and thoughtfulness as a demonstration of gratitude and the relationship eventually comes to an end is because the person who was being spoiled never realized that the reason the person was showing them such love and attention was because they were trying to set an example of how they themselves would have liked to have been treated but never was.

- Sometimes you can feel like it seems like everyone is against you and you just can't seem to get along with anyone. Take a moment to examine what is the only common denominator with all the people you seem not to be able to get along with. If you're truthful and you find the answer is you, then one day you'll learn that the only person you can change is yourself. When you change it will seem like everyone else finally changed and it seems like you can get along with almost everyone when the only person that really changed was you. Wow, what great things that can happen to us when we just work on ourselves while we are waiting for everyone else to please get themselves together. If you want to know who will give you the most problems throughout your life, look in the mirror! There are a people that you know that are very thankful that I pointed this out to you because you never would have received it from them.

- When a man or woman comes home, they don't want to come home to a Doctor, Lawyer, Accountant or Business owner. They want to come home to someone who is all women or all man first and has them as their first priority as a husband or wife and then is a master at being a mother or father to their children. All the other things they bring to the table are just added to the cake. That's why someone can have someone with all those titles and end up in an affair with someone who has none of those professional qualities, but is very good at just being someone that is a master at knowing what a man or woman likes and how they want to be treated. You can have the best of both worlds as long as you understand that balance is the key to life."

- Sometimes the hardest thing in your life is to know which roads you cross and which ones you burn without destroying good relationships. Some men and women will find themselves in a relationship with the outside appearance of having a whole and happy relationship, but behind closed doors lack the skill to walk out what it takes to have the real thing because they failed to know the difference between likeability and compatibility. Just because two people can see a lot of things in each other that they like, it doesn't make them compatible. There are a lot of people that love each other, but it wouldn't be good for them to spend their lives together.

- When people feel they need break away from you let them go. Your destiny is never tied to someone who leaves you and it doesn't mean they were a bad person at all. It just means that their part in the story of your life has come to an end whether they added something to your life or drained something from it. Its just how life is.

- **Relationship Tip.**

Someone you love is asking themselves, have you been with me so long that you never figured out why I spoil you and love on you so much? It's because they are trying to show you how so desperately they wish you would treat and love them the same way!!! When you tell people how awesome this person is to you at some point you should add what you do in return. One sided love affairs don't last long. It's a good way to end up by yourself.

- Don't make the mistake of thinking something in your relationship is alright with your partner that you know really ISN'T ALLRIGHT. You give place to a slow buildup of resentment in the person you are in relationship with that in time will build up to a point of an explosive confrontation one day and you will wonder where did all this come from? Just because they stopped complaining doesn't mean they stopped noticing. They are quiet because they're privately hurt and disappointed that you don't respect them enough to make what's important to them just as important to you don't talk about it, just change.

- Why do you think most people in troubled relationships allow themselves to stay that way longer than they have to? It's because they never have the nerve to have a conversation about how they REALLY feel about each other and the things they really like and dislike. Why? For fear the other person won't be able to handle it and just simply at least make a commitment to get better so they continue to be quiet about things that really bother them and let silent resentment build inside that will one day potentially explode. So much can be avoided by talking from a place of truth with the intent of peace and TRUE happiness. I know these kinds of comments won't get much public response, but I'm satisfied you saw it and maybe will consider it.

- The only thing about the people you come across your life that changes will just be the faces. There will always be people that either add or take away. Make sure you know the difference and have more that add to your life then those that take away

- Intentions without actions is what has reduced goals you could have achieved to just a thought. Potential is what you could be but you're not yet. Only action = Manifestation.

- It's not what you go through but what you grow through that makes you a seasoned and mature person in life. If you grow through life right there should come a time in your life when you become worth more because of the things you know than what you can do.

- It's a dangerous thing to be in a relationship with someone who does everything for you and they get little to nothing in return from you. When this happens, you could end up losing a very good thing that you may not ever come across again and you were the one who made your partner vulnerable for someone else who saw from a distance how they were treating you but your partner was left lacking themselves. All another person has to do is to start treating your partner like they were treating you while thinking you were going to return the love and attention but never did. Don't ever take you being blessed enough to have a good man or a good woman for granted. When they stop begging for your attention and paying less attention to you, there's a reason. They have decided to make their own needs and happiness a priority instead of yours. IF YOU TRULY LOVE AND WANT THEM, YOU BETTER SHOW THEM WHILE YOU STILL HAVE THAT CHOICE BEFORE YOU DON'T

ANYMORE. I've seen many a man and woman think they would just find another one but never did again in their lifetime.

- When I see people, who have just gotten out of a relationship and go right back into another relationship it tells me one of two things about them. Either they were already seeing the other person they got right into a relationship with while they were with the previous person or they really didn't care for the previous person as much as they made that person think they did. It takes time to get over the shock of being separated from someone you say you really care about and love. The easier it is to go to the next person, the less you really cared."

- LEARN TO APPRECIATE WHAT YOU HAVE BEFORE IT BECOMES WHAT YOU HAD.

- Someone left a message for someone they were in a relationship with to read. It read: "Thank you for always being there for me when I needed you most. Thank you for all the warm hugs and kisses, letting me lay my head on your shoulder, the soft, I love you, always encouraging me and telling me how wonderful I am." The person it was addressed to read it and then called and asked, are you sure you meant to send this to me? The person who sent it said, "yes, it was all the things I hoped you would do for me at some point in our relationship, but you never did. At least when you get home, you'll understand why I'm gone."

DOES YOUR PARTNER SPOIL YOU? I WONDER WHY?

Someone you love is asking themselves, have you been with me so long that you never figured out why I spoil you and love on you so much? It's because they are trying to show you how so desperately they wish you would treat and love them the same way!!! When you tell people how awesome this person is to you at some point you should add what you do in return. One-sided love affairs don't last long. It's a good way to end up by yourself.

- Remember, when you are in a troubled relationship, especially when children are involved, the worst thing you can do while trying to work things out, is to get involved with someone else. It's hard to make a [what's just right decision] in most cases because your interest is now divided, the ones who will be affected the most won't even have a voice in your decision, which are the children. P.S. Here's a bit of advice: Anyone who knows you're in a relationship, trying to work through some things, and they entertain you on the sly – they're taking advantage of your weakness. If you fall for it and leave the one you're with for them, they will eventually leave you for someone else because at the root of who they are as a person. They do not have any true character or integrity. Truth be told, you are likely not the only person they are seeing NOW. A lot of men like to pursue women who are hard to get. Not because they care, but to prove to themselves they can. Don't ever restrict yourself to the only thing you know about a person is simply what THEY tell you. Do your homework with other people.

- Many men and women are attractive enough to get themselves married, but are not mature enough to know what it takes to stay married. You have to develop into being a good wife or a good husband by experience and educating yourself in the area of relationships. You both will need the humility and a willingness to develop into it. If you're reading this after the fact, then honestly accepting that neither of you gave each other the time needed to grow into a spouse. If you're truthful, you just may not have been prepared to give in the relationship what was going to be needed is a great place to start. That will buy you Grace since it's already been exposed that you both may have advertised yourselves as being ready for something that you were unable to deliver on so soon in the relationship

- If you're ever in a relationship and someone feels they have to choose between you and someone else, trust me, you DON'T want to be the one they choose. As soon as you hit a rough spot, the person who chose you will feel they made the wrong choice. If someone feels they care for someone else as much as they care for you, LET THEM HAVE THE OTHER PERSON, because you should be made to feel like you're in a class all by yourself.

- If you don't feel secure in your relationship, ask yourself this question. How much more would someone else have to do for the person you're in a relationship with to be doing more than you are? If the answer is, not much, you may have reason to be concerned.

- Most people end up in bad relationships because when they first met someone they acted like they didn't see what they saw. They then acted like they didn't hear what they heard. People will always show you what you will have to deal with once you get into a relationship with them. Make sure you stay out of the denial of what they are really showing you about themselves. Pay attention to details. The difference between you being happy or heartbroken will be in your ability to read between the lines of what you hear and see right before your eyes.

- It's tough being in a relationship where you find yourself remaining close enough to someone to make sure they get what they need, but you keep yourself remaining far enough away from them in your heart so that you don't get hurt. If you're in a relationship where you can't give your whole self and knowing that person is giving their whole self to you, then you need to get counseling to fix it so that you don't remain in a state of being married to someone you're borderline divorced from mentally, you just don't have the papers to show it.

CHAPTER TWO
Singleness

- When you put your list together for the qualities in a spouse you're looking for there ought to be two lists. One for what you are expecting and one for what you bring to the table. Remember, you need to look for husband or wife material because boyfriends and girlfriends are only there long enough for you to discover. They can look good on the outside, but you may not be able to live with what's on the inside of that person.

- Don't expect a higher catch in a man or woman than you're able to deliver to them in yourself.

- There's a big difference between making a person feel like they are being appreciated rather than tolerated or desired rather than being annoyed with. Remember, what goes around comes back around to you.

- Marry a person you like as much as you love them knowing you will always at the least be friends. It's possible that one day the fire won't always burn as hot and you feel as you do now. But at least you know the deepest you can fall with someone you vowed to care for forever is still someone you still like as a person and you're still friends. Forever is a long time to be unhappy with someone you no longer even like.

- A person's commitment to you is only a promise until it's tested. If you're dealing with people that make promises that never reach the state of a commitment then you may be witnessing previews of coming attractions with those people if you get into a long-term relationship with them.

- Thinking about getting married? This may help...

When most people think about marriage, they have seen in their mind a picture of a little white house with a white picket fence around it and their spouse pushing them on a swing, just smiling and laughing while the children play in the grass. Sorry to tell you this, but there is no such thing awaiting you from the beginning already finished.

The truth is, you will build it through sacrifice after sacrifice, compromise after compromise, interaction by interaction, tear by tear, one conflict after another, through self-examination after self- examination, embrace after embrace, and from thinking you love someone to finding, maybe you didn't as much as you thought. Or maybe you'll find out just how deeply you do love them.

Be encouraged, it is very possible to build the house, the fence and the swing, one board, one foundation, one paint stroke at a time over a period of years into just that.

Understand it's a process and not something that is already waiting for you. This way you won't be so disappointed because it didn't happen after the first year.

That way the children can happily play in the grass as they witness and partake of what you both worked so hard at to now have something that's truly real with each other.

- Most singles always want to know how do I find a good mate? How should we go about seeing if we are the one for each other, and is now the time to pursue marriage? What gets most of them in trouble from the start is that most of the time, not knowing, they put the carriage before the horse. What I mean by that is you need to back up to when each of you left your parents' house and ask yourself these questions;

    o   What kind of product did your parents put out in you when you left the house?

    o   Also, once you left the house, what did you write on the history of your life yourself?

o   How many relationships have you had? How many good? How many bad?

o   What are some of the scars other people left on your life and how many did you leave on other people's lives? Did you take any, just you time to get over relationships that didn't work out even though you were convinced at least a couple of them would?

You need to think about these things because, these are the very things that will have a profound impact on what kind of a relationship you will be able to have with anyone, even if the person you meet is the best person you could have ever met in your life. You will deal with them most of the time through the filters of your own personal experiences. If you don't stop to think about some of these things and the person you're considering for marriage doesn't do the same thing, these are the very things that will come out in future marriage counseling sessions that you will find that are the root of your marriage problems. These are a couple things a couple needs to explore before they look for THE ONE or let THE ONE find them. Marriage counseling is what I do, so take it from me. I have just given you a cheat sheet to get off on the right foot to having a long-term happy relationship. Take some time to evaluate yourselves and each other's past and you will have a clearer idea of what you both really bring to the table to work towards a REALLY HAPPY MARRAIGE.

- **EMOTIONS**

The most important decision you will ever make is who you marry. This will be the most important decision you'll ever make because you will choosing a person that once you have a child together you will be linked to them for the rest of your life whether you stay married to them or not. You are actually choosing the parent of your children and the grandparent of your grandchildren and they will be stuck with them no matter if they're a good person in the end or not. And so will you. Do your future children, grandchildren and yourself a favor and not let your emotions overtake your common sense and leave you stuck with long lasting consequences, but happiness.

- Show me you love me by having sex with me with the risk of getting pregnant by someone who will either encourage me to get an abortion or may not claim the child as theirs and can't help take care of the child even if they do? Tell them to put a ring on your finger and you can have all the sex you want and anytime you want it. Don't let your temporary emotions to someone reap your long-term consequences for not only you but also possibly the child that may come from a moment of pleasure.

Just a thought...

- It's hard to accept when someone has already disconnected from you, but you have yet to disconnect from them. Sometimes, when you try so hard to hang on to someone that has broken your heart and you're willing to work with them to save the relationship but they turn their backs on your out stretched hand, LET THEM GO, because you may not have any idea WHO AND WHAT you are being saved FROM, and WHO AND WHAT you are being saved FOR until you remove them from your life and move on with your life.

- Never bypass a person's reality to embrace their potential when considering a relationship. Always deal with first things first or you will face the reality of what happens when you put the carriage before the horse.

- *Dear Single People,*

When first meeting someone don't ever be so trusting of the other person that you limit what you know about them to only what they told you about themselves.

It's wise to pay attention to people who knew them before you did or at least make a note to self to see if someone else has seen some of the things you see.

Do this especially if you really like the person because you may not be able to trust yourself to pay attention to what they're really showing you for fear of losing them so you'll convince yourself that they'll change or you can change them.

- *Why do most men stay single so long?*

Because most of them think higher of themselves than they ought to!

One of the main reasons is because they have so many more choices of good women to choose from as opposed to women having to choose from a pool of fewer good men. Both men and women have their list of what kind of spouse they're looking for, but the fact is both men and women should have two list available.

Men and women's list include things like:

Young and fine, tall, physically fit, good job, good credit, money in the bank, nice car and comes from a good family among other things.

Question,

what does a person with all those qualities get in return in you???

Pause and think about that and then make sure you are working on you to the point that if you are blessed to find a person like the one on your list you yourself will become a blessing and a gift to their lives and not a curse and disappointment.

It's easier for a good man to find a good woman then it is for a good woman to find a good man.

Why?

Because the pool to choose from is larger for the man.

Ladies, if you happen to end up with truly a good man, always know you are in the minority and definitely not the majority. Make sure you appreciate him, make sure you let him know just how much you do.

Remember this, another woman will if you leave that door open because most women know one when they see one by watching how they treat you, but you can't even see it.

Men, if you happened to be blessed with truly a good woman and you find you really don't have the skill to give her what she truly deserves, commit to learn by study and finding a mentor or role model you can learn from by just observing their life on how a man treats and serves his woman to the point that other women are envious that she has a man like you and I'm not even referring to sex.

- Having sex in a relationship only takes up 1% of 1% of the time couples spend together in a day, but you have found common things to do the other 99.9% of the day.

The 99.9% will determine not only what kind of relationship you'll have together, but how long it will last, not the 1% of 1%.

- It takes a real man to be a man when it's time to be a man and it takes a real woman to be a woman when it's time to be a woman and there are some out there.

- No matter what kind of person you portray yourself to be openly you are not who you really are until you're all by yourself and no one else is around. When those two people match you are not a hypocrite.

Why single men shouldn't be so afraid to marry a woman with children.

There are so many men that look to marry a woman with no children because of what they went through with a single parent and the holes it left in them because of the lack of the right role models and the struggles they may have experienced as a result of not having both their parents.

You would think these men would be the first to want to make sure that fatherless children wouldn't go through what they went through by not letting that be a tiebreaker.

You also get the chance to fill a great void in some child's life because maybe God loved them so much, he gave them you.

They need to remember at one time it was them and their single parent that good men were passing by because of that same kind of thinking.

- *The consequences of soul ties and to many lovers while we were just having fun.*

The discovery and reality of the danger and consequences of too many lovers in your life before you find the one you commit the rest of your life to and who also commits the rest of their life to you. You may find that you thought you were done with your past, but your past may not be done with you!

It's amazing how many times we thought we found the love of our life only to find we didn't.

There are so many things in our life we wish we could do over. Even still, we can get past it and have a prosperous and loving life with the one we love and end up with.

- When preparing for your wedding day, don't spend so much time preparing for the wedding, that you fail to prepare for the marriage. People aren't coming to the wedding to see a show, but they and God are coming to witness the both of you say a vow of words to each other that you promise to never break as long as you live. Spend more of your time preparing for that. Can you handle that? If not, cancel the wedding.

- *Did you break up with your partner last night and got another one today!!!*

When I see people, who have just gotten out of a relationship and go right back into another relationship it tells me one of two things about them. Either they were already seeing the other person they got right into a relationship with while they still were with the previous person or they really didn't care for the previous person as much as they made that person think they did. It takes time to get over the shock of being separated from someone you say you really care about and love. The easier it is to go to the next person, the less you cared."

No one should be quick to get into a relationship with someone else while they still have the residue of the person they just broke up with on them.

- *A love affair that is doomed from the beginning*

Anyone who is dating or pursuing someone that you know still loves the person they just separated from needs to think again.

Your persistence of "I just have to have him or her" will never earn you the respect and love from the one you're pursuing because they know that you know they weren't your first choice from the beginning.

Eventually that reality will break your heart.

Back off while you still have the strength to do it and check on them in about a year or so they may be well worth the wait. Either you will be glad you did or you will wish you had. P.S. And don't get upset at them because it was you that was trying to cash in on the weak and emotional state you knew they were in when you made your move.

Single ladies,

Keep your bank closed until the man has a ring on your finger. It's the best way to keep from making the same mistake twice leaving another child without their father in the house while they grow up.

It amazes me how so many women can be in a relationship with a man while sharing the most intimate parts of their bodies with that man and get in a financial situation just because a family emergency came up. Your lights were turned off and she lets her boyfriend, who she just slept with drop her off to an apartment that has NO electricity.

When asked why she didn't let her boyfriend know just what was going on, she replied, I don't feel comfortable asking him for money.

ARE YOU SERIOUS???

You just gave him the best of everything you have to someone you can't be transparent with when you hit a bad spot? Maybe you really don't have the kind of relationship you think you have. Never commit the milk before he buys the cow.

- When looking for a mate, one of the things you're looking for in that person is a person who COMMANDS your respect because of the contents of their character and how they carry themselves. That's different from a person who has to DEMAND your respect. There are a lot of people who are in love with people they have LOST respect for, but when you have a person you have a LOT of respect for, because of the kind of person they are and how they carry themselves, a lot of times you can grow to love that person even though you didn't think you loved them all that much in the beginning.

SOME WOMEN WERE TAUGHT HOW TO PROTECT THEMSELVES FROM A BAD MAN BUT NOT HOW TO APPRECIATE A GOOD MAN WHEN SHE FOUND HIM DAVID E GOODIN

SOMETIMES YOU HAVE TO TAKE THE FUTURE OF YOUR LIFE OUT OF THE HANDS OF SOMEONE ELSE'S HAND AND MAKE A DECISION FOR YOUR OWN LIFE BECAUSE IT'S THE ONLY WAY YOU CAN STILL SALVAGE YOU.

DAVID E GOODIN

Dating someone who does not want to be married when you know you want to be married it's like buying a very fancy car that you can only drive on a dead end street.
-David E Goodin

CHAPTER THREE

Parenting

- As a single parent it's not a good thing to bring different men and women in and out of your children's lives. You are training them at an early age that its ok to have multiple partners that never make a lifetime commitment to them. You should tell your children you are seeing someone, but they can't meet you yet because they have not proved to you that they are worthy to meet your child or children yet. It leaves your child feeling valued and special instead of asking you Mommy, where's Bobby, then Al, then Ron, then Ken, or Daddy, where's Mary, then Michelle, then Kelly, and then Janet. It leaves them confused and with a wrong example of what to expect when they enter into a relationship themselves.

- The responsibility of being a woman and Guardian of The Birth Portal that brings children into this world.

Most young women will someday have a child and she must protect and be a good steward of when she gives someone permission to enter the birth portal knowing the possibilities that conception may take place at any given time. You open the gate no matter who it is or what the circumstances.

Most young ladies think when they open their portal they are showing an expression of love or making love. There is no such thing as making love when it comes to sex. Sex doesn't and isn't for making love. You don't make love. It's a feeling you develop into or make when you choose to love someone in spite of how they treat you. Sex is for making babies or reproduction. Unless the man you let enter has protection every time it's just a matter of time where the woman is going to find herself pregnant.

When that happens, what kind of benefits will the child have because of who you opened yourself up to?

1. When they are born will they have both parents there when they arrive?

2. Will they go home with both parents?

3. Will they even know who their father is?

4. Will they see their father?

5. Will they feel their father changing their diapers?

6. Will they experience their father getting up with them in the middle of the night?

7. Will they experience their father rocking them to sleep?

8. Will they think it's a normal thing for their father to be feeding them?

9. Will their father be there to rejoice as they take their first steps?

10. Will it be their father that teaches them to ride their first bike?

11. Will their father be there when they're up all night with a fever?

12. Will their father be there to take them to the emergency room if they ever have to go for any reason like an ear ache?

13. Will their father come to their school to check on and support them while in school?

14. Will their father be involved in their sports or activities while they're in school?

15. Will their fathers have developed the kind of relationship with them where they feel they can come to them with not only their problems but for validation and encouragement that can only come from a father?

16. Will their father provide an environment for them to grow up in as far as where they live and how well they live that will set a bottom line standard for that child's expectations for the type of environment he will set for his family?

17. Will that child if a boy grows up wanting to be like their father and if she's a girl wanting to marry someone like her father?

These are just a few questions that will come as a result of how well a woman protects and Stewards her gateway through the portal to life. Do your children a huge favor and make sure your choices end up being a blessing to them and not a curse. And remember they will live with your choices, not theirs.

You will either be glad you did or wish you had.

There a lot of things that happened to us because we just didn't know. But once we knew better, did we do better?

There is great responsibility that comes with having a child long before you actually birth one.

- I look at my son, and I see who I was, but when my son looks at me, he sees who he might become, a powerful revelation for us both. Something to think about.

- When your child is turning 18 soon and you ask them; now that you're grown, what are you going to do with your life and what do you want to become?

In their reply, don't let them turn to you and say, I'm going to do exactly what you've prepared me for Mom and Dad, be thankful for you both, but do Better!! You taught me how to make a Life for myself, but you didn't give me an example of how to actually enjoy it. You taught me how to keep a roof over my head and to get an education, but you never taught me by example about LIFE, relationships, how to resolve differences in a relationship and how to truly love someone or how to respond to someone that shows me that they love me. I'm going to do exactly what you and Mom prepared me for, so thankful for all you sacrificed for me, but I want to learn how to enjoy life along with how to truly love someone and how to appreciate it coming from someone else along with how resolve differences with people who are dear to me throughout my life.

Question, is it possible for your child to respond this way?

- *Parents can learn new skills that their parents did not have that can still benefit their children today.*

At some point parents have to take the responsibility of learning new parenting skills that we didn't get at home while we were growing up so we don't continue to release our children out into the world as damaged goods because of what we didn't teach or model before them while they were still at home.

Ask yourself this question, knowing all the things about yourself you know about yourself, including those things you know no one else besides you and God knows about you that if your child grew up and one day met someone just like the real you and the example you modeled before them, would you want your child to marry that person? If the answer is, NO, then change some things about yourself, now.

- *This was a conversation with one of my son's, Jullian, a few years ago.*

One of the things I shared with my son last week, that I should have shared with him 30 years ago, was that after having 6 children by 4 different women and not having a father explain to me the possible consequences of sex was the reason you should wait until you're married to have sex.

We are taught that when we have sex, we make love.

There is no such thing as making love because you can't make love, you have to learn how to love.

Then learn how to receive love from someone. Then learn how to give expressed love to someone else, in the manner they need it expressed to them. You learn after you grow up, if we ever, do as men, that when you have sex, you don't make love, but a lot of times we just make babies. There are a lot of women that thought they were showing a man how much they loved them by having sex only to be left with a baby, but without the man that they thought they were showing how much they loved them. When you have sex outside marriage with no long-term commitment expressed and have children as I, your father did, you really create SINGLE MOMS with no man in the house just like I did with your mom.

Julian grew up one day to tell me to my face what he really thought about me not being there for him as a whole and as a young man how it was growing up without his father in the house.

That was a hard pill for me to listen to and swallow.

I really hoped he learned what not to do from me.

He had no choice with the hand that was dealt to him.

But I told him, "If you repeat what happened to you, and to your children, shame on you son." You really didn't learn a thing. It's possible your son will one day grow up to have the same conversation with you that you had with me. Knowing you, I've learned you've learned a lot and thank God that won't be the case with you.

Now of course this is just my opinion and not a one size fits all point of view because there are so many situations going on.

People can have their own opinions to which they most certainly are entitled to have like myself.

I've got 50 years of experience and 20 years of counseling in these situations. I have more facts than just an opinion.

I told him, "I love you son."

For those who can hear the message behind the message I hope you too can benefit from just a few of my mistakes growing up without my father and just trying to find my way through life like so other men today.

- Fathers it's never too late for your children.

It's Never too late for a father to make up for not being there for his children or at least try. - Kage Goodin

Almost fourteen years ago with nine children and after realizing you don't raise all of your children the same because they aren't the same. They all are individually different and now all the children are grown and gone except one. I asked one of my sons who was about twenty-five or twenty-six a question.

Keep in mind this was a son where I left him, his brother and his mother while he was only five years old for another woman.

This also was the son that as growing up his brother told me that if you really wanted to make his brother mad, call him David Goodin because of the things he went through because his father wasn't there while in his eyes his father was busy taking care of someone else's children while he and his brother suffered watching their mother struggle to take care of them. All of my children have a relevant story they could tell.

I used to call him and sometimes he wouldn't take my calls for weeks.

As we were relocating to Jacksonville, he happened to be over to the house, and I asked him this question.

"What do you do when you realize you weren't there or didn't raise your children as well as you could have, but now they're all grown except one and gone out on their own?"

He looked at me and said, "YOU START NOW, DAD, which is all you can do and all we can ask for."

These words would end up being the bridge for reconciliation with my children over the next thirteen years. It would allow me to enjoy the relationships with my children we have today even though each one of them can always be better.

I did start there with just trying to be there for them either in advice or financially whenever I could especially since my children never asked for much, not even money.

I love all our children and I've learned to value and treasure each individual relationship with each one of them being as precious to me as the other. They are all different and at different places in their lives and I dearly love each one of them right where they are without comparison. I treasure whatever relationship they allow me to have with them without drama. They all know I don't do drama at all.

That son that gave me that advice thirteen years ago might not think it to be a bad thing to be like the man his dad is today and he doesn't get upset when you call him David Goodin anymore.

FATHERS START NOW!! START TODAY!!

- Years ago, one of my sons tried to impress me with pictures of all the ladies he had since those were the kind of memories he had of me. I told him, "Son, I found out the life I lived before you was wrong and that I hurt a lot of good women. If you want to impress me with what kind of man you are, show me you can love and be true to ONE woman, marry her and have all your children by that ONE woman and stay with that One woman and your children. That's a man son."

- *Dads, you can't raise a child from a distance. you have to provide more than money and weekend visits.* For a parent to say I helped raise my child you have to ask yourself a series of questions like,

- Was I up through the night with them as a baby on the nights when they refused to go to sleep? Did I help so that their mom could get some sleep?

- Was I there when they suffered through an ear ache as you as a parent watched helplessly knowing there was nothing you could do to help them?

- Was I there with them while they were going through the agony of teething.

- Was I there to feed them their first spoon of solid food?

- Was I there when they took their first steps?

- Was I there to hear the first time they said mama or dada?

- Was I there to drop them off for their first day of Day Care?

- Was I there to drop them off for their first day of school?

- Was I there to make sure they did their homework before they went to bed?

- Was I there the day your daughter discovered she was having her first cycle?

- Did I visit the school to meet with the teachers to show you we're involved with your child?

- Was I at their school functions for sports and other things?

- Did I contribute to them beyond what child support ordered you to do?

- Was I there to take them to the emergency room when they had to be taken there?

- Was I there celebrating their significant birthdays like, 13, 16 and 18?

- Do I know their favorite color?

- Do I know their best friend?

- Do I know their dream car?

- Did I take them to their first day of work on their first job?

- Do I even really know your children?

I had six children by four different women and missed out on a lot of these points and they turned out to be great children, that I love dearly.

But I know how they turned out was not because of me being there, but in spite of me not being there I have to give that credit to their mothers. When I grew to know better, I did better and now have good relationships with all my children, thank God.

As fathers we have to push to do more than the minimum because when your children are grown they will tell you exactly how they feel about how you were there for them whether good or bad like mine did me.

When you get to a point you can do better, then, just do it. You'll either be glad you did or you'll wish you had.

As a parent while raising my children and looking back and seeing how imperfect I was and so many things. I could have done better, I am so thankful to God that my children forgave me and gave me another chance.

- *A Life Lesson From One Of Our Daughters*

A few years ago, when we were very successful in a business one of my daughters came into my office and needed to talk to me while I was on the phone.

She knew when I put my hand up that means not now and go back out of the room. I used to do this often because I was so deep in my work.

One day as I was on the phone and she came in and I put my hand up for her to turn around but she kept coming, and this upset me. As I was still talking on the phone she leaned down and began to write something on my Calendar. I paused and asked her what are you doing?

She said, "I just made me an appointment on your calendar since that's the only way I'm going to get a chance to talk to you" and then she turned and walked out the door.

To this day, I pause for my children no matter what I'm doing or who I'm doing it with.

- *Will what we are modeling before our children lead them to be blessed or cursed???*

Consider that when a child is born they come with a blank canvas, with no previous history of anything, but we as parents get to determine what sounds, pictures and daily activities will become normal in the life of that child by the daily environment the child lives in.

The parent will determine what the child will have going through their ears and eyes, and what will get down into their heart and spirit.

Therefore, what comes out of the child's mouth will be a sum total of what they've heard, what they've seen and after a while got down into their heart and became normal to them. These are the things that frame a child's mindset and how they view the world and people they will one day have to live with. If we don't like what we see in our children, hopefully it's not too late to change the programming.

Sometimes when I see a homeless person or a teenager getting a life sentence for murder, I think to myself,

this is not how their life started because they, just like my children the day they were born, everyone was excited to see them, and just like my children, they too came with a blank canvas and someone began to write on the history of their lives.

Evaluate what you're putting before your children's eyes, and what you're letting get into their ears and eventually gets into their hearts, because it won't be long before it comes out of their mouths which will direct a course of direction for their lives.

Lord knows, I wish I had known this before all my children were grown because I would have done much, much better.

It's only by The Grace of God that our children are the awesome children that they are today because only he can make a crooked stick straight and put Humpty Dumpty back together again.

It's never too late to start now.

- As a parent, while raising your children, don't miss out on the opportunity to instill and model the value of being others minded and a person of integrity, a person that honors their parents and a person that does not judge, but gives the benefit of the doubt to all. Why? Because it's easier to train a child than to correct an adult and almost impossible to start imparting those things into their lives when they are 30 instead of 10. *You will be glad you did or you will wish you had. So will the spouse and children they end up with.*

- At some point, parents have to take the responsibility of learning new parenting skills that we didn't get at home while we were growing up so we don't continue to release our children out into the world as damaged goods because of what we didn't teach or model before them while they were still at home.

- Don't take having a parent or parents that are still alive for granted. Don't ever take your parents still being alive for granted. Before she passed, my mother would tell me to send her roses while she could still smell them, and not to put flowers on her grave. Also tell her I love her while she could still see the words coming from my lips, rather than tell everyone how much I loved her when she's gone. I'd do anything and everything to do those things for her just one more time. Mayme Jo, I miss you.

- YOU HAVE NO MORE CHILDREN!!!

You can want a stress and trouble-free life for your children, but as parents it's hard to accept that we just can't make choices for them. One day you will have to face a hard truth that YOU HAVE NO MORE CHILDREN and that you now have ADULTS that have to make the same decisions you had to make yourself for them to get on the right path for their life. Make sure you model a life that shows you too were able to transition from a person who used to think like an Irresponsible child to a mature and responsible adult. There should be a difference in your thinking and lifestyle than that of when you were a child.

- *Parents, if you died today, would your children and family have to scrap just to bury you? I hope not because it's not their responsibility, it was yours!!*

No child should have to figure out how to put their parents away with dignity, but it happens all too often and is a great burden on a family. Children should know if their parents have enough insurance to put them away with dignity and at no cost to them (or their church). Children ought to ask their parents if they have it and where it is and if they don't have any, you better get some on them because either you'll be glad you did or you'll wish you had. When a parent passes there should be no need for money to go FROM the children simply because there should be money passed TO the children simply because they're the child. Even if it's a couple thousand dollars each. It should be something.

I worked for mine and they need to work for there's such a sick mentality. Or nobody left me anything. Wow, really? Be the first in your family to do the right thing and start a new tradition for your children and grandchildren.

- When living together, why does the man always move in with the woman instead of the woman moving in with the man??

- Why did I spend 16 years living with three different women??

Mainly because while growing up, it's all I saw from my parents and a lot of other families around us. It was just normal and so when I got married and had a woman on the side, it was just normal even when we separated I move directly in with my girlfriend I had on the side while still married and wondered why my first wife was tripping.

Took me a long time to realize that EVERYTHING PRODUCES AFTER ITS KIND. CHILDREN DO WHAT THEY SEE, NOT WHAT THEY'RE TOLD.

Any man going into a relationship should at least have the desire to be able to cover the household bills on his own income without needing his wife's.

That's not always the case these days and I understand that, but it should be his natural desire at least. Some situations we get ourselves into we just didn't know better or know how to learn how to do better.

Common sense is the highest level of intelligence.

Once we know better, we have to strive to do better with the examples we set before our children.

I am still seeing the consequences of the life I lived before my children in my children to this very day.

Shame on me if I never grew into a better example that was inspiring and just left them with the old one.

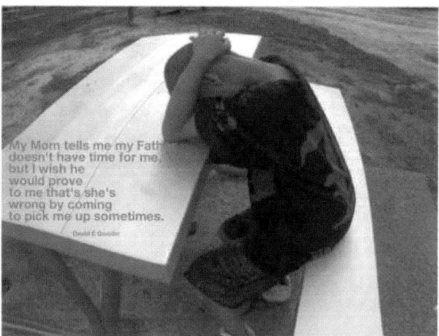

CHAPTER FOUR

Marriage

- Ask yourself a question; am I always complaining to my mate that they don't give me the kind of attention and love I deserve? Ask yourself another question; am I expecting a harvest on a seed I don't sow myself?

- Many times, marriages break up for reasons other than the final straw that broke the camel's back. A lot of marriages don't necessarily end because of what event actually happened at that time, but for reasons that weren't said and unspoken buildups over a long period of time.

- Ask yourself this question; how much more would another man or woman have to do to be doing more for your husband or wife than you are? If you examine yourself and the answer is not much, yet your spouse is faithful knowing they're being shortchanged maybe the reason they are still able to be faithful is because they're more spiritually mature than you and faithful to the relationship vows they publicly made than you are.

- My Pastors, Michael and Connie Smith have discovered the secret to pursuing the Vision in Ministry God gave them and have longevity in Ministry as a couple at the same time. They have learned to pursue and please each other as a husband, and a wife, as much as they desire to pursue and to please God. It is this that has made a mark in the lives of me and my family that cannot be erased.

- If your mate asked you to describe to them the kind of person you thought they were, how would you describe him or her? Have you ever told them in detail what you think about the qualities they possess in detail and how happy and thankful you were because you are the one who gets to benefits from them? Or you don't because you don't want them to get the big head so you leave them open to hear it from someone else, and when you find out someone else is telling them things that you should have been the one telling them you're upset and angry when it was you who left the door open to it in the first place by not giving them something everyone needs; confirmation of just knowing how much they're loved and appreciated.

- You should be the first to compliment the beauty, gifts, and wonderful personality of your mate and not the second, third or fourth. It's a sad thing when the praise, respect and expressed love for the kind of person they are comes more from the outside rather than those in their own household and the person they sleep with every night

Are you and your partner communicating or just talking?

When someone is talking to you about something very important to them, it is very important that when it is your turn to listen that you have Selah moments, which means, pause, and carefully think about that.

When they talk and you talk right back, you never gave yourself the chance to ingest what they said, therefore you were never able to digest it and respond in a manner that gives the person you're talking to the impression that you truly heard them and exactly what they were trying so hard to get across.

Effective communication cannot be done in a blender atmosphere. It can only be effective in a crockpot atmosphere.

Sometimes you have to slow the conversation down from 80mph to around 30mph to really hear, comprehend and respond to the subject and the motive, purpose and intent in which the concern was shared.

Selah, pause and carefully think about that.

- Even though some of the things your spouse does doesn't interest you, Wisdom says, make sure you assure them that what's important to them is also important to you when you see them excited about something they enjoy by being excited too. Now that's a very wise partner that leaves no place for someone else to appear they are more compatible for them than you.

- There is a reason why 90% of a prostitute's clients are married men. And they have the same REPEAT customers. It isn't the sex. It's the fact that they know how to tell the man what his wife doesn't or won't. They understand the concept of validation and affirmation. Most women are so busy to show a man how much they know. Instead of trying to validate, to their man, how much he knows. They don't understand the wisdom and power behind that. They also don't understand the doors that they leave open, for another woman, by NOT doing that."

- When on the verge of divorce or breaking off a relationship and you both as individuals decide to really put more effort into making it work, remember, the next 14 days are crucial to that ever happening. Why? Because you're still so close to the edge of what got you to the place of calling it quits and the first little thing that happens that you don't like, you'll throw your hands up and say, I'm done!!! So, what do you do? You pay close attention to your own-selves, that's what and not the other person.

A lot of times, not all of course, when marriages end up in divorce, whatever happened that triggered the last straw was not the real reason things went sour. A lot of relationships break off not because of some things that were said, but things that weren't said and kept inside for a period of time until it was just too much to bear anymore.

When you get to this point and the two of you talk some things out and decide to give it another shot please know one or both of you are going to aggravate the other in some way because it takes a little time to break habits so you both have to purpose to give each other a real chance and not go off on the person the first time they make a mistake. And as you see them trying not to do the things that aggravate you, compliment them on the effort you see them putting forth and this will encourage them that then really can do this.

Commit to 90 days and revisit because during the first 30 days you're to close to the edge and anything can make you feel you're wasting your time when actually you may not be. You didn't get to where you are overnight and most things won't be fixed overnight, but at least know you gave things a fair shot.

- How can a marriage go from the best thing that ever happened to us, to becoming our greatest disappointment in just 5 years? One neglect at a time until it has become a habit that has become so normal to you that you are now annoyed when your spouse wants to talk about it. This is the beginning for a couple that is already divorced, but they just haven't filed the paperwork yet.

- *The most fulfilling kind of love a person can ever experience.*

Most people go through their lives longing and searching for some person to come across their lives that would pour out a never ending and overwhelming love towards them that would continue throughout their lifetime and then some and I can truly understand a natural desire like that. But the greatest kind of love that one can experience is not a love that comes to you, but one that is able to freely come from you.

There is no greater or more liberating feeling of satisfaction then to be able to pour out all the feelings of love that are inside of you that have been subconsciously on hold desperately waiting to be released towards someone else.

Especially with the tested assurance that the love and emotions you are willingly and so excited to express towards them will not be misused or taken advantage of since you have waited so long to pour out onto someone you truly love. Find two people like that and you have found Utopia.

- *To Christian Wives And Husband*

If your Husband or Wife was not saved, could he or she be won by the relationship you say you have with the Lord and by how you carry yourself and how you treat and communicate with him and the children?

Ask yourself one day; when you are older, what would your life be like if it's solely based off the love, compliments, compassion, and care you have given your spouse or children and family over the years?

What kind of seeds are you sowing in those relationships now on a daily basis that in the latter years of your life when there is little to no sex and your good looks have faded, your mind isn't as sharp as it used you be and your health is not that good, and instead of being able to help someone, you are the one who needs help and you are left to live in the harvest of what you have sown in your relationships with your spouse, your children and your family?

Give them your best now, not your leftovers. One day you will either be glad you did, or wish that you had.

[Pause, and carefully think about that today]

GOD HELP ME PLEASE
I DON'T WANT

TO TALK DOWN ON MY HUSBAND
LIKE MY MOTHER DID TO MY

FATHER BUT I GOT IT FROM HER!
I WAS TAUGHT HOW TO PROTECT
MYSELF FROM A BAD

MAN BUT NOT HOW
TO APPRECIATE A GOOD MAN WHEN

I FOUND HIM DAVID W GOODIN

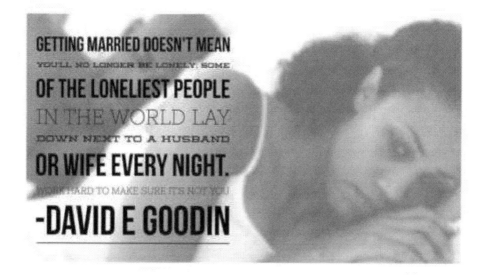

CHAPTER FIVE
Wisdom Nuggets

- Remember, when people feel they need break away from you, let them go.

- Your destiny is not always tied to someone who leaves you, and it doesn't mean they were a bad person at all. It just means their part in the story of your life has come to an end, whether they added something to your life or held it back. Its just how life is sometimes. The only thing about the people in your life that changes will be the faces. There will always be people that either add or take away. Make sure you have more adders.

- Choose to be a person of true humility because PAIN WILL TEACH YOU WHAT YOUR PRIDE WOULDN'T LET YOU LEARN.

- If we truly are a spirit and spirits live eternally and there really is a Heaven and a Hell then every person who ever lived is still alive. It may just be a question of what address they are at.

- Sometimes you can meet your purpose and destiny on the road you took to avoid it.

- Don't confuse assumption with validation.

Seasoned Wisdom

Solomon lived a life looking at the lives of others and his own life always taking notes and sharing with others.

People ask how do Cynthia and I have so much knowledge on life in general and relationships.?

Every day of my life I learn something new about myself, both from my past and present. I also learn from others as I come into contact with them. I take mental notes of learning from their experiences.

Also, we've been blessed to experience the full cycle of family, which is living to see one of your children become a grandparent. We should have learned a few things by now, but even now we're still learning from things we could have done better and what's for us to learn even today.

No matter where you are in your life at this present time, don't ever confuse a season in your life as being the sum total of your life. There are many seasons to a person's life. Some good, some bad, and some ugly. They are called seasons because they all pass. Don't believe it?

Look back over your life and see how many situations you thought you were stuck in only to see them pass. Maturity is getting to the point when the unknown occurs and you don't know what to do, you can look back over your shoulder and see the things you overcame. It will give you the faith to go forward without knowing where you're going. It's just a season in your life; it's not the sum total of your life. So, take a deep breath and LIVE.

- Let your life be the kind of life that was all about OTHERS, and you will live the kind of life where you want for nothing for yourself. You'll have a life where there is nothing missing and nothing broken in it. Now that's a good life.

- It's a tragedy to have lived a life where you felt like you were on top of the world after climbing out of the shadows of the gutter, only to have never experienced true happiness, love, and fulfillment because no one taught you how to live in the dash of your life. Balance, is the key to life.

- How you feel about yourself privately will eventually be displayed by how you carry yourself openly.

- What you find yourself focusing on can greatly influence your decisions and how you physically feel at that time. To the degree of your focus will be the degree of its impact whether it is positive or negative.

- The more clearly you make your goals; the clearer the paths to obtain them become.

- Any habit you continue to permit will always increase. Habits never decrease on their own good or bad.

- Love is an action word.

- You cannot correct what you continuously deny exist. If ten people told you that you're drunk, more than likely, you're drunk. If ten people tell you, you have an anger problem; you probably have an anger problem.

- When you decide to no longer condemn yourself for past failures, you will position yourself for a future where the sky is the limit. Realizing your mistakes will allow you to go forward, condemnation will keep you stuck in the guilt of your past. Let it go, dog, let it go!

- It's most interesting how often pleasure follows things that are in order and when things are out of order it seems so hard enjoying some of life's pleasures. Remember, Order is the prerequisite for true enjoyment and success.

- When around successful people you have to purpose in your heart that you will always be the best listener in the room. This will posture you to receive nuggets of wisdom that can change your life forever. Make sure you're not the one in the room who has the most to say, because you can't learn while you're the one who's always talking. Some of us need to demonstrate how smart we are by being quiet. When around successful people they may realize, every time you open your mouth you demonstrate to them how much you really don't know.

- If you have a mentor in your life they can recognize people in your life that are good for you and the ones in your life you need to purge from your life.

- A SIMPLE BUT DEEP TRUTH. When we repent to God for something that we did wrong, that's not when he found out what we did. He was there with us watching while we were doing what we were doing. God didn't learn anything new about us. We learned something about ourselves.

- If others had to eat from the fruit of your life, what would it taste like? Oops, you can't answer that. The truth can only be answered by the people that are presently eating from your fruit.

If you're not satisfied with the answer you can start today by making it better.

- Encourage Yourself in The Lord. Sometimes when you don't know what to do and there is no man to guide you or advise you, that is the season you'll confirm to yourself that you trust God for real. Always know the farthest you can fall, is in the arms of a loving God.

- You're right where he knew you'd be today because he never makes provisions for us in a place he knew we wouldn't be. It's impossible for God to mismanage our lives, so relax with great expectations of what the next season of your life is about to present to you. A God directed life never takes you down, it always takes you up.

Be Encouraged Today.

- Don't always be so quick to tell people what you know, because it will never speak louder than what they see you do.

- *Does fruit always confirm you heard from God?*

You have to know the difference between when and after you step out on what you "think" God is leading you to do and seeing fruit after you step out and "think" it to be a confirmation of what you stepped out on. You have to ask yourself if the reason you have fruit after stepping out on something is because of the God directed life you live, which causes everything your hands touch to prosper. If this is true, you can bear fruit and still be out of the will of God for your life. How will we find out which is which? One will be short lived and the other will continue with longevity, confirming the will of God for your life. This is just my opinion. There is always more to a revelation.

- Sometimes we can't see the forest for the tree. Don't let yourself become mentally absent from the people who love you that are in your present by longing to be with someone in your past. Then your left to wonder why you can't vision a future with the one you're with that loves you now. Only fools trade the thought of being with someone else in the past for someone right in front of them that they can touch and hold and love now!! LET THEM GO DOG, LET THEM GO!!!!!

- **Ask yourself a question.**

Am I always complaining to my mate they won't give me the kind of attention and love I deserve?

- **Ask yourself another question.**

Am I expecting a harvest on a seed I didn't sow myself?

- **Tell the truth and shame the devil.**

Takes a man to be a man when it's time to be a man, and there are few because a lot of women handicap them.

It is rare now days to find a good man who is a caring person, has a good job, his own car, his own place, and no children. Especially, when there are so many women who will compromise being cared for, let him stay home while she's at work, use her car, stay at her place and give him children he doesn't have to stay and take care of.

Hats off to the sharp brother who gets himself stable before he invites someone else into his life or helps bring a child into this world and never leaves them or their mother.

Ladies and Gentlemen even if we made mistakes we have to do better once we know better.

A conversation between me and my son Kage...

Me to my son, Kage: I don't know what in the world is going on with your generation!!

Him to me: Dad, it disgusts me when I hear your generation complain about a generation you created!!!

Me to him: what in the world are you talking about??

him to me: when you and mom and your friends were

smoking the weed, snorting and smoking the coke, taking the pills and drinking, while we as little kids were sitting on the couch or playing on the floor or in our rooms, what did you think was going to happen to us??

Did you think that we were going to grow up and go to Harvard University?? really ??

Me to him: Silence

Some of you reading this post still have time to make sure none of your children say this to you

WE HAVE TO DO BETTER!

Father's Day, is a day of giving honor where honor is due and deserved. To some wives and children, it is a day of joy and excitement, but to many, it brings about many other mixed emotions.

For a father there is no greater feeling than seeing something you produced grow up into someone great and awesome. To be someone that people love and respect based off the kind of awesome human being they are; even if it's not a result of you being in their lives it's in spite of you not being there in their lives.

I meet both men and women who rave about being a daddy's girl and men that are excited about spending time with their fathers.

I've also had men and women tell me recently they don't have any idea who their father is or that he died, is in prison, left the family while they were young or they see them from time to time. You also can in many cases feel and hear in their voices the determination to overcome the void they feel in their lives.

I realized that I didn't give enough young people credit for the inner strength and determination to make something great out of themselves in spite of what they had or didn't have. I commonly discovered that the inner strength and determination came from having a strong and determined single mother, who in some weird way, (like my mother was when I was growing up) was able to play both roles in a way that their children didn't even know they were poor or lacking. Somehow these women ensured their children did not feel like they missed out on something or was short changed on feeling loved.

A lot of us have been blessed with fathers that deserve all the gifts, praise and love we can bestow on them and there are many. But more than not, this day is a reminder of a void that as a child you had to press down and hide somewhere in your soul because no matter how well you were able to go on with your life and make something great of yourself, deep down inside there is something missing; the love, validation and feelings of protection that come from having a father around?

I see many fathers who love spending time with their children and invest a lot of time and love into their children. Some are working two and three jobs and attending as many of their children's activities as they can. These are shining examples of good men that have built an honorable image where their sons want to be just like them and their daughters want a man just like them.

If you have one like this or you are married to a man like this then please GIVE OVER THE TOP HONOR WHERE HONOR IS DUE because you're truly blessed more than most. Don't ever take having a man or father like this for granted.

I also see fathers who just hang out day after day saying they're looking for a job, no car, no address of their own, no interaction with their children, giving no support towards their children, and year after year it's no better, but the children are growing and still have needs daily. It makes you wonder how are these children able to still make something of themselves in spite of not having their fathers in their lives?

In many cases, the father not being there is the child's driving force. It pushes them to overcome and make something of themselves and one day they end up taking care of their mothers for the sacrifices she's made her whole life.

The other reason, more often than not, is the fact they had a strong single mother who didn't have the option of waking up and saying, I'll stay home today because I'm so tired, no such thing as you didn't come up with the rent, no such thing like you don't have the money for the electric bill, no such thing like you didn't provide food for today, no such thing like I can't pay the car note, no such thing as I can't stay up with her children late in the night when they're sick, no such thing as not finding a way to get to the school to check on progress of her children, no such thing as her children not having money for field trips, no such thing as not having money to get growing children new clothes, no such thing as not having her children hear the words, I love you and you can make something out of yourself because you're great and wonderful and beautiful.

She doesn't have the choice to do or not to do!!!!

So, todays Father's Day and some of us cannot wait to show our appreciation for the awesome fathers we have been blessed with. Lord knows I hope I'm one of them because I wasn't always, but when I knew to do better, I did better.

To others it's another day of revealing what we didn't have, but also what we did have which was and is, a powerful, loving, hardworking and sacrificing single mother, who if she wants to can double dip on this Father's Day because she had to master both roles and there are not enough words to articulate her sacrifice for her children.

Happy Father's Day with a balance.

- Riding through a neighborhood where houses run $500,000 & up, I noticed something. It's rare to homes that have brand new cars even though there were two or three in the driveway, most of them were at least 10 years old or older. It looks like they pay them off and keep them with no car note to pay. The rich stay rich by acting like they're broke and the poor stay poor by acting like they're rich.

- I am amazed at how many men and women over 50 still tear up from the effects of growing up without their fathers no matter what the reasons were. Most men don't reach out to their grown children because they feel they've lost the right to do so. My father was 80 when I spent my first overnight stay with him and it was worth every bit of me reaching out to him. Reach out to that Mother or Father if it's in your heart to do so. You may end up filling a hole in your life that only that one human can fill.

- A blessing from the Lord for your life will never become a curse for others in your life that are connected to you. Don't ever step into a new season of your life before first tying up loose ends on the present season of your life where people or commitments are concerned. God will never bless you with something that will cause you to compromise your character and integrity.

- Character, integrity and balance is the key to longevity in success, life and relationships.

Transitioning from personal friendships to embracing a life with your spouse.

I find a lot of people don't know the true purpose of friendships in their lives. Many people meet the love of their life and they postpone or abort relationships with their friends. They figure they are with the future parent of their children and are going to build a life together for themselves and their children. True friendships are priceless and very few people have more than one if they have that.

Most people confuse friends with acquaintances, which is why they are always disappointed when these friends are not REALLY there when most needed.

Once you get out of your teen years and come to the end of your twenties you may be lucky enough to meet the person you'll spend your life with. Once the two of you have made it clear you are going to spend your future together, you both should begin to slowly move your friends at arm's length in communication and time spent and begin to gravitate more towards your future spouse even though the two of you may not have made it official yet.

How well you navigate through this process will have a lot to do with if the relationship officially gets to the level of engagement ESPECIALLY WITH FRIENDS OF THE OPPOSITE SEX. Hint-Hint.

I'm not saying get rid of all your friends immediately. I'm saying as you begin to prioritize in your everyday life the time spent with these friends should begin to DECREASE and time spent with the person you plan to spend your life with should INCREASE!!!!!!

As a single person most friends are just meant to be a bridge between being single and when you've found THE ONE!!!!

You no longer spend significant dates and times with your friends anymore, but with your future lifetime love.

If you fight to continue to do the things with your friends like you have always done you will find the other person start to back pedal out of the relationship. This is because they understand it is a preview of coming attractions and they are right because this will be an issue in the relationship. No matter what you tell them, THEY WON'T BELIEVE IT and why should they when they see how hard it is for you to understand a common-sense adjustment.

I've seen many people lose a lifetime companion because they don't know how to put friends in the proper perspective. They END UP ALONE over friends that are no longer in their lives.

If you can't prove to a person they are exclusive in the pre-engagement stage they aren't going to take your word that it's going to change once you are engaged or married. These are things one should pay special attention to before they ask someone to marry them and especially before someone says yes.

Will you still have friends in your life and do things with your friends after you're married and have a family? OF COURSE YOU WILL!!!!!!

But they will be the friends that understand this process and will still be there for you because they understand. Honestly, they can't wait for the day THEY ARE IN YOUR SHOES. They already know they will have no problem adjusting with you, when they now have a spouse and family to focus on building a life together with.

Don't let friendships abort what you've been waiting on all your life. Don't end up living your life alone only because you didn't understand that most friends are just a bridge between two seasons of your life!

Either you'll be glad you did or you'll wish you had.

What does stretch marks on a woman's body really mean?

After thirty years of counseling, I've had many men ask me, is there anything to help stretch marks on a woman's body? I've also had many women ask my wife if there is anything that get rid of stretch marks because they don't like the way they show up on their body.

I have a thought on this that I'd like to share and it's just my opinion and nothing more. When a couple is young and in love and they have yet to have children or maybe even if she has children already this still can apply. When a couple meets and falls in love and decides to get married and have a family they both because of their youth have flawless bodies because he is looking fit and she has in many cases a smooth shined body with all the right curves even though some may be larger or smaller than others.

As they decide to now have children, a wife says to her husband, I want you to look carefully at my body and how nice and smooth it is right now because I'm getting ready to make a sacrifice to give you children that's going to cause it to make some changes where I won't quite look the way I do at this moment. She says to him, I want you to promise me that as I continue to sacrifice my body WHILE YOURS PRETTY MUCH REMAINS THE SAME, I want you to promise me that when you happen to pass by women who may not have had children and you see that they still have a body that could be as flawless and smooth as the one you are looking at now as you look at mine, please do me this one favor. Promise me that you will remember me as I am now when you have the temptation to compare someone else's body who didn't make the sacrifice I made with mine with how I'll look then. Promise me please!

When a man sees the stretch marks on his woman's body that she has because of the sacrifice she made to bare him children and knowing, his body made no such sacrifice, OUT OF SHEER LOVE AND GRATITUDE, HE SHOULD KISS EVERY SINGLE ONE OF THEM EVERY CHANCE HE GETS.

- *Transitioning through a life altering event in your life*

Throughout our lives, a few things are certain. One of those certainties is the fact that life will deal you a few hands where you don't have the answers and it'll be at a time in your life when you need answers the most.

- It could be one where you just moved from one city to another city that you really don't know much about.

- It could be a divorce or separation from someone you've been with for some years.

- You could have been downsized suddenly and you weren't prepared for it.

There are three phases you will go through.

1. A year of adjustments
2. A year of stability and
3. A year of leverage

It takes a year to adjust to a new life in a place where you know little to no one. How and where to look for a job, a place to live, where are the good schools, where are the stores? It takes a year to just adjust mentality and emotionally no matter if it's job, relationships or anything else that is life altering in your life.

After going through that first year of Adjustments you now move into the year of stability where you pretty much have gotten your life into a routine and you start to see some stability ahead. You no longer are in doubt about the move or event that has affected your life, but you are now moving forward with purpose.

Going into that third year you are no longer adjusting or trying to find stability, but now you are ready to leverage yourself and make some moves for your future. You know what side of town you want to buy a home, and what schools are best for your children, what roads are best to take to your destination and now you can advise others. Now you are making choices for your future and no longer adjusting.

The problem most people have with a life altering event in their life is expecting in one year what it may take three to accomplish. and they stay in a state of frustration wondering what's wrong with their life?? Slow down and embrace the process and *you'll either be glad you did or you'll wish you had.*

- *Encourage Yourself In The Lord Today*

Sometimes when you don't know what to do and there is no man to guide you or advise you, that is the season you'll confirm to yourself that you trust God for real!

You're right where he knew you'd be today because he never makes provisions for us in a place he knew we wouldn't be it's impossible for God to mismanage our lives, so relax with great expectations of what the next season of your life is about to present to you.

A God directed life never takes you down, it always takes you up.

- What happens when you have wrong people in your life? When wrong people start leaving your life wrong things stop happening in your life. People in your life will be remembered for one or two things, 1.) The problems they help solve in your life, and 2.) The problems they help create in your life.

Make sure you know the difference.

- Don't always counsel yourself about you!

The most dangerous person to confine yourself to counseling with is yourself, because it is almost impossible for you to tell yourself the truth about you. The truth about you and how you really treat and relate to people can only come from other people, not you!

- Until you let go of your past, what's waiting for you in your future can't arrive. sometimes you are truly blessed in your life, but if you haven't moved on from your past, you can't even see it.

- When people break away from you, let them go! Your destiny is not tied to someone who leaves. you and it doesn't always mean they were a bad person at all. It just means their part in the story of your life is over, whether they added something to your life or not. Its just how life is sometimes, people come and people go.

- It's not hard to find the right person at any given time. All you need is two people who have purposed in their heart they are going to be a person that is always going to do THE RIGHT THING concerning the other person and considering their own needs as secondary to the needs of the other person's needs. Now find a person like that and purpose to be a person like that and the two of you will have found the right person.

- Don't complain about things that are constantly bothering you when the only reason they exist is because you just won't make a decision. Sometimes you have to make some decisions, accept the consequences of those decisions, and don't look back.

- Your character is easier kept than recovered. You can spend your whole life developing and building a reputation of having unquestionable character and in one wrong act or decision spend the rest of your life trying to recover it and sometimes, never able to. This leaves you with the regret of what could have been but never was because you compromised the most valuable treasure a person can possess, which is their character. You don't want to be the one to testify that passions, pleasures, the pursuit of gain or money and positions, you would trade in a moment for the recovery of your reputation of having unquestionable character and integrity

- Someone once said, if I died and could come back as anyone I wanted to be, I'd like to come back as the person I could have been, but never was. Since you're still alive and you're reading this, work on being that person you know you really could be while you're still alive.

- Wise men speak, because they have something to say. Fools speak, because they just have to say something.

- There is no such thing as cruising in life. You are either progressing or regressing. People that think they can cruise through life as it comes eventually find themselves stuck in life or going backwards, because even to maintain cruise speeds you have to press down on the gas sometimes to keep going forward or you're going to slow down and come to a halt. Life never stands still for anyone. In life you are either progressing or you are regressing.

- Don't ever underestimate the validation that can only come from a father to his son or daughter. Praise that comes from others is fine and good, but it is of great necessity and importance when validation and praise come from your father. Few things in life will give you more joy and personal self-fulfillment.

- When wrong people start leaving your life wrong things stop happening in your life. People in your life will be remembered for one or two things, the problems they help solve in your life, and the problems they help create in your life.

- Your future financial success will be determined by what you are willing to do without today. A penny saved, turns into a penny earned. So go on a penny-pinching spree and increase your income without even getting a raise. How much money did you spend today that you knew you really didn't have to spend? Until we get a handle on our spending, our dreams will always be in the distance and never in the now.

- You cannot rise above the level of company that you keep. Want to get a sneak preview of your future? Take an inventory of the people you hang around. It's a proven fact after a 40-year study that only 2 out of 10 people break out of the mold of average because they understand this principle. Are you one of the 2? Take a look around you first before you answer.

- The problems with most people's goals are not that they set a goal so high they were unable to reach them, but because they didn't set any, they reached them every day as they regressed.

- Don't ever confuse discipline with a habit. Discipline takes a conscious effort to birth a habit, and a habit is an unconscious behavior that requires no effort at all. Strive for discipline in the areas of your shortcomings until they become the habits in your life you desire.

- Don't ever measure how far a person has come in their lives by the measure of your opinion and how far you have come in your life because you may be thinking of yourself higher than you ought to.

- A [Procrastinator] is one who puts things off until a window of opportunity closes on them and the excuses they use many times are just lies that have been camouflaged by reasons of why they haven't moved on the opportunity yet, even though they know getting in motion would move their lives forward. So, don't remain at the front of a step that was never taken, telling yourself you'll do it tomorrow and tomorrow has become years and you're still procrastinating.

- A person can learn about life two different ways. You can learn by wisdom, or you can learn by experience. Wise people learn from other people's experience without having to go through them.

- Everyone has the right to speak, but you have to earn the right to be heard because in most cases a person can only receive from you to the degree of respect they have for you as a person.

- You will find your Destiny after a period of years of making just the right amount of combined right and wrong decisions.

- You can want a stress- and trouble-free life for your children but you just can't make choices for them. One day you will have to face a hard truth. The truths of realizing you have no more children. You now have adults that have to make their decisions like you had to make for them to get on the right path for their life.

- Comparison is like Cancer. It starts out small but if you don't cut it off it will soon lose your own identity.

- One of the worst things that can happen in your life is to get to the end of your life and wish you had done more with your life. Remember, you only get one shot at it and will you be left with the fruit of what you did with it, or what you didn't do with your life. Where ever you are in your life is a direct result of decisions YOU made or YOU didn't make to get wherever you are at the end of your life

- Think about this. When King David sinned with Beth-Sheba God sent a man to David to ask him a question. God said ask David, does he know he slept with her before my very eyes? Remember God can see the blackest ant on the blackest night under the blackest rock and every vein that runs through his body. When we repent to God, that's not when he found out what we did, he was watching us while we were doing it.

- Remember, God has a habit of placing some of his greatest future impacting Saints for the Kingdom of God in Satan's own back yard with him not knowing one day they will become informers that will come out of his world and be washed by the water of the Word and be able to go back into Satan's world and yet not be of his world and compel others to come out of his world.

- Remember, because you are a spirit, and spirits don't die, remember, everyone who has ever lived, is still alive. It's just that they are at two different addresses. No matter how you feel about Heaven or Hell, those who have passed, are all one accord, because they exist and live in the truth of that opinion. There is no argument between them anymore. We debate, while they know. You too will get the chance to see if your opinion of what you believe is true. I'm going to live my life like there is a Heaven, just in case there is a Hell. It's to big of a gamble to just roll the dice.

- No matter where we find ourselves in life it is a direct result of decisions we either made or didn't make throughout our lives. We can always trace where we are in life back to a decision. If those decisions have landed you in a bad place then all you have to do is make different decisions and they can still take you to a good place in life.

- You should appreciate what you have before it becomes what you had. You don't miss your water until your well runs dry.

- All you can do is all you can do, and if you have done all you can do, then that's enough because that's all you can do.

- A person who doesn't like anyone telling them what to do will always be a person that thinks everyone else is doing them wrong.

- You can tell just how much of a future you have by just observing what you do on a daily basis. Consistently and persistence lead to a life of success.

- Remember there is no such thing as tomorrow because you will always only have today because when tomorrow comes it will still be your today. Maximize your today's.

- There's a big difference between making a person feel like they are being tolerated rather than appreciated or annoyed or desired.

- *God, can you use me one day even if I was,*

Conceived in a rape?

Had my name changed three times before I was seven?

Even though my father lived five minutes from my house but never picked me up until I was nine years old?

Even though I dropped out of school in the ninth grade?

Even though at 18 my girlfriend got pregnant the first time I had sex?

Even when the next girl I had sex with got pregnant the first time too?

Even though I left my first wife and moved directly in with another woman the same night?

Even when I left her for another woman?

Even though I was a part of a number of abortions?

Even when some of those women who had those abortions never got pregnant again?

Even though I was a drug addict?

Even though I was a drug dealer?

Even though I did so much of drugs my body was breaking down so bad it almost took my life?

Even though I sat in a car for two hours drinking Hennessy and coke and smoking weed with a gun in both pockets waiting for a guy to drop my girlfriend off and was going to unload both guns into him before he could get out of his seat?

Even though I had six children by four different women?

Even though when I came to church I was living with my girlfriend?

Even though I didn't grow up going to a church?

Even when I did go to church I had to look in the table of contents to find the book of Genesis?

NOW LORD, CAN YOU REALLY USE SOMEONE LIKE THAT???? (and you know that's not all of the story because you're God) Let me look over my life and see if you really were or not WOW!!!!! YOUR GRACE HAS BEEN SOOOO GOOD TO ME.

- Remember you can't be plucked from God's hand but, you sure can choose to walk away from it. The power to choose is always in your hands not his. The question is, where have your choices taken you?

FREE ADVICE IS NOT ALWAYS GOOD ADVICE!!

- One of the easiest areas for most people to voice their opinion is in areas they have no personal responsibility, accountability or consequences. This is when they are convinced they have the answer to your problems. Just remember, it cost them nothing, but could cost you everything."

- Pause and think about that while their lips are still moving.

- Some people have the potential to fly and succeed but never put themselves in a position where they had to fly or fail and therefore never did experience the potential they had inside them all the time. They took the manifestation of their potential and their dreams to the grave. Step out now so that won't be you!!!!!

- Remember you will find your Destiny after a period of years of making just the right amount of combined right and wrong decisions.

- The Gospel should not be preached as if it's hard or complicated. Jesus made it simple by breaking it down into stories. Everything He said was simple and anything that wasn't simple he didn't say. When the Gospel gets too complicated for the uneducated and the unlearned the teaching is off. People must get understanding and be able to comprehend so they can apply what they understand to their everyday lives. If you're in a church where you truly don't understand what's being preached and your life is not changing for the better, find one where the preaching ministers to where you are in your life and the issues you're trying to overcome in your life.

Clue = if there's stuff in your life that you know isn't right, but you want to get it right, when you go to a church and sit through a service and aren't convicted by the Word preached to get it right, you are simply in the wrong place for you and what you need. You can waste time at home.

David E Goodin
The most important decision a woman will make in her life is who she chooses as her man because she's also choosing the father of her children whether he will stay with her or not. Because there are so many broken women there are to many sharp men who can see her brokenness and be cunning enough to make her think she's choosing him when he's controlling the whole situation all the time. Women have to slow down and really do their homework so that they don't wake up one day and find themselves in situations they feel they can't get out of. The man you choose really can make or break you. 30 years of counseling:)

CHAPTER SIX

Blended & Step Family Tips

When coming together in a marriage and one of you already have children, or maybe both of you do, the thing that is taken for granted the most is that the children and the parents will all accept the dynamics of the new family arrangements under the same roof with an objective attitude and things will work out fine, right?

I mean, it is, what it is, right?

No, it doesn't.

When blending a family, most times there is to high an expectation and not enough information or pre- engagement Blended Family counseling with a counselor that has experience in what you are headed for.

Stepparents, just because you have the title now means little to the step children. You have to earn their respect and not demand it. The only reason they are a stepchild is because they have had a loss. They lost a parent living with them. It usually takes a child 2-3 years to finally accept a version of family they've never seen.

You earn their respect by first becoming a friend. Get to know them as a person. As time goes on, they will begin to treat you like their aunt or uncle which means, they now look at you as a part of their family. Then you'll find them referring to you with their friends as their Mom or Dad.

It's a process.

You will find yourself very disappointed if you as a stepparent if you expect all three phases the night of the wedding or in the first year.

Blended & step-family holidays tip when children are grown.

One of the things my wife and I had to face about four years ago is that all our children are grown and are either married or are in their own relationships which means, we no longer have exclusively on holidays anymore. What a reality for us to have to face!!

Normally we would plan out the holiday and automatically expect the children to come to our house like they have all their lives when they were available to do so.

Then we noticed some would like to spend the holiday with their other parents or stay home with their own immediate family and swing by their in-laws house and others would have to leave our house early to go to their other parents house or a boyfriends or girlfriends parents' house.

Cynthia and I had to face the reality that things had changed and we needed wisdom how to process and deal with it. Then we got this wonderful idea where we would have our holiday get togethers A WEEK EARLIER. This way we could have the children and grandkids at our house for Mother's Day, Father's Day, Thanksgiving and Christmas and then on the actual holiday everyone was free to do and go wherever they choose. It has been a real burden remover for us and whoever stops by on the actual holiday is always an extra blessing.

This Sunday we are having our Christmas at our house and all the children living in Atlanta will be here and next Sunday everyone is free to do as they please and sometimes they will switch up and be with us both weeks but they know there is no pressure on them at all while they've trying to make everyone happy.

This will work with younger children also This has been a huge thing for us to transition into, but it works for us and may not for everyone.

- **Blended family tips....**

Just one reason why premarital blended family counseling is so vital to the success of a blended or step-family marriage. Things to consider while you're still single with no children.

- Whenever you get married with a child or children you will face the reality that getting married with a child or children is not the same as getting married and neither of you have children. Why? Because when you go into a marriage without children you start out with only two parents. When you go into a marriage with children, you start out with at least three or most of the time four parents. This happens because the outside parent in the triangle will either in most cases get remarried or have a significant other who will also have influence in your child's life or in your marriage.

- Here's 10 things to consider concerning blended family's marriages and children.

    1. Your children won't be raised in two different households where they have to be subjected to four different people they have to submit to who may have four different views on how a child should be raised because they come from four different families and had eight different parents raising them with each of them having their own views on how they were raised.

    2. You won't have the third eye or the third ear in the marriage where you check out how you treat your biological children as opposed to how you treat your stepchildren and who you spend the most time with.

    3. You won't judge the tone in which your spouse speaks to your children as opposed to how they speak to their own children.

4. You won't have to consider another parents outside your home when raising your children.

5. Your child or children won't be leaving your house every other weekend to go stay at some other house that may have different values in their house than you have in yours.

6. You're not going to hear words uttered like, YOU'RE NOT MY MOTHER OR YOU'RE NOT MY FATHER!!!!

7. You're not going to hear the words, I WANT TO GO LIVE WITH MY MOTHER OR I WANT TO GO LIVE WITH MY FATHER!!!

8. You won't have to wonder if a parent is going to contribute financially to the raising of the children.

9. You're not going to have to deal with the possibility of the children having sex with their stepbrothers and stepsisters because they aren't REAL brothers and sisters so they don't look at each other the same way they would if they were.

10. You'll never have to utter the words; CAN WE JUST SPEND TIME WITH JUST OUR BIOLOGICAL CHILDREN SOMETIMES???

These are just a few things that most people going into a marriage with children don't talk about or consider going in because most don't know these are questions they should ask. You have to counsel with someone who knows what questions to ask for you.

- When coming together in a marriage and one of you already have children, or maybe both of you do, the thing that is taken for granted the most is that the children and the parents will all accept the dynamics of the new family arrangements under the same roof with an objective attitude and things will work out fine, right? I mean, it is what it is right? No, it doesn't. When blending a family most times there is to high an expectation and not enough information or pre- engagement or blended family counseling with a counselor that has experience in what you are headed for.

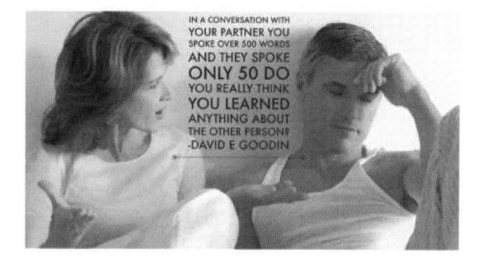

IN A CONVERSATION WITH YOUR PARTNER YOU SPOKE OVER 500 WORDS AND THEY SPOKE ONLY 50 DO YOU REALLY THINK YOU LEARNED ANYTHING ABOUT THE OTHER PERSON? -DAVID E GOODIN

ALL MEN AND WOMEN DIE,

But Not All Men And Women Lived.

PAUSE, AND CAREFULLY
THINK ABOUT THAT

Today. David E Goodin

CHAPTER SEVEN
Prosperity

Total prosperity for me and my family god really is good.

Over the pass twenty-seven years I have had two men in my life teach me about true prosperity in life. Pastor Creflo A. Dollar and Pastor Michael T. Smith.

I didn't grow up going to church so when I met Pastor Dollar I had nothing to unlearn, but came with an empty cup ready to be poured into. I thank God over the years he gave me the greatest gift anyone would ever give me which was to teach me to read and know the Word for myself to such a degree that if God forbid he fell I wouldn't fall by the wayside because I knew the Word to be true for myself. Also, if he did fall the only thing I would have done is to be there for him like he always was in my life when I fell.

All my life I never tithe or gave anything to church people because I didn't trust them. I started tithing off $6.00 per hour in 1986 while married with eight children at the time not knowing one more was on the way one day.

I was taught it did little good to tithe without living as a true Christian not only openly but also behind closed doors. It took a while to develop into that second part but I think other people will tell you I work hard at it.

I don't know or care much about what other's opinions are about tithing, but ALL I KNOW IS TWENTY-SEVEN YEARS LATER: My wife and I are blessed to be healthy in our bodies and our minds. We live in the house that we wanted. We live in the neighborhood we wanted. We have jobs doing what we most love to do which is ministering to the needs of people. We work for the most awesome bosses on the planet. All nine of our children are healthy. All thirteen of our Grandchildren are healthy. All of our children are self-sufficient requiring no help or aid from us doing things they love to do. We don't get the phone calls that no parent wants to get in the middle of the night. Our children are good people and we hear it from other people all the time. They love giving back to us.

We have never stopped tithing to this day and never will.

NOW THAT'S THE PROSPERITY I WAS TAUGHT!!!!

- **A TIP FOR BUSINESS**

Make sure that while you're making money you save and put away all you can because the people who get it and then loose it all are the ones who think it's always going to be coming in!!!!

The people who are the most successful in business are the ones who hung onto a job for as long as they could and the growth of their business FORCED them to quit their jobs.

To many people do it backwards by first quitting their jobs and going full time business and not having enough money put aside for the bumps that will come with having your own business.

Always treat people like THEY are more important than the business and you will ALWAYS have people in your business.

- If you want to be assured of being successful, 1.) FIND A NEED AND FILL IT and 2.) BE THE ABSOLUTE BEST AT WHAT YOU DO WITH YOUR PRODUCT AND SERVICES.

PEOPLE ALWAYS SEEK OUT THE BEST OF
SOMETHING!!!!!

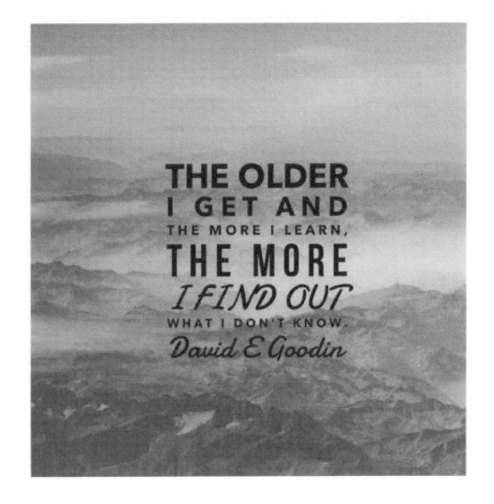

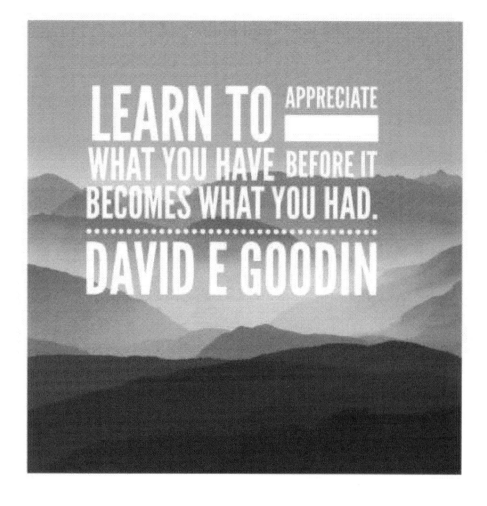

ABOUT THE AUTHOR

David E Goodin

David E Goodin was born in Xenia, Ohio to David M Goodin and Mayme Josephine Anderson as a result of date rape. He spent the first nine years of his life in Xenia and then moved to Elyria, Ohio until 1982 when he would move to Atlanta, Georgia. David has been married to Cynthia Goodin for Thirty-Three years. They have nine children between them as David had six children by four different women while his wife Cynthia had two children by two different men and then adopting a niece when she was twelve years old. There were a lot of things he learned growing up in a single parent household and also having step-parents while at the same time having a lot he didn't learn, but over a period of many many years would learn a lot of things the hard way and his wives and children would be the ones most affected by what he knew and didn't know but his ability to look back over his life and not only learn from his mistakes but to use himself as an example of what to do and not to do has allowed him to land in an incredible season of his life where God has done great things through him throughout his life until this very day.

He has been a counselor for the past twenty-five years, He ministers in the prisons, he has mentored over two hundred men and lives his life to encourage whoever comes across his path. This book has so many things that can help so many people because it speaks to many situations a person can find themselves in throughout their lives. When you have this book at your disposal it's like having 24/7 access to a counselor or a wealth of wisdom in your back pocket. He is a master at saying and articulating things that people in relationships think about, but don't want to talk about and saying it in a way that no one is confused about what he is saying. You are guaranteed to know a lot more about relationships than you know now once reading this powerful book of wisdom and insight. Enjoy.

Made in the USA
Columbia, SC
01 March 2025

54538259R00057